SEP 2011

LI

Dear Parent:

Congratulations! Your child is taking the first steps on an exciting journey. The destination? Independent reading!

STEP INTO READING® will help your child get there. The program offers five steps to reading success. Each step includes fun stories and colorful art. There are also Step into Reading Sticker Books, Step into Reading Math Readers, Step into Reading Phonics Readers, Step into Reading Write-In Readers, and Step into Reading Phonics Boxed Sets—a complete literacy program with something to interest every child.

Learning to Read, Step by Step!

Ready to Read   Preschool–Kindergarten
• big type and easy words • rhyme and rhythm • picture clues
For children who know the alphabet and are eager to begin reading.

Reading with Help   Preschool–Grade 1
• basic vocabulary • short sentences • simple stories
For children who recognize familiar words and sound out new words with help.

Reading on Your Own   Grades 1–3
• engaging characters • easy-to-follow plots • popular topics
For children who are ready to read on their own.

Reading Paragraphs   Grades 2–3
• challenging vocabulary • short paragraphs • exciting stories
For newly independent readers who read simple sentences with confidence.

Ready for Chapters   Grades 2–4
• chapters • longer paragraphs • full-color art
For children who want to take the plunge into chapter books but still like colorful pictures.

STEP INTO READING® is designed to give every child a successful reading experience. The grade levels are only guides. Children can progress through the steps at their own speed, developing confidence in their reading, no matter what their grade.

Remember, a lifetime love of reading starts with a single step!

For Dev and Rachel
—D.R.S.

For my daughter, who is my everyday heroine
—P.S.

Visit us on the Web!
StepIntoReading.com
www.randomhouse.com/kids
www.marvel.com

Educators and librarians, for a variety of teaching tools, visit us at
www.randomhouse.com/teachers

ISBN: 978-0-375-86776-7 (trade)
ISBN: 978-0-375-96776-4 (lib. bdg.)

Printed in the United States of America
10 9 8 7 6 5 4 3 2 1

STEP INTO READING®

STEP 3

IRON MAN™
ARMORED ADVENTURES
PANTHER'S PREY!

Adapted by D. R. Shealy

Based on the episode

"Panther's Prey" by Cyril Tysz

Illustrated by Patrick Spaziante

Random House 🏠 New York

Iron Man hovered outside
a skyscraper window.
He was following
a group of evil scientists.
They called themselves A.I.M.

(1275998747600034360000)

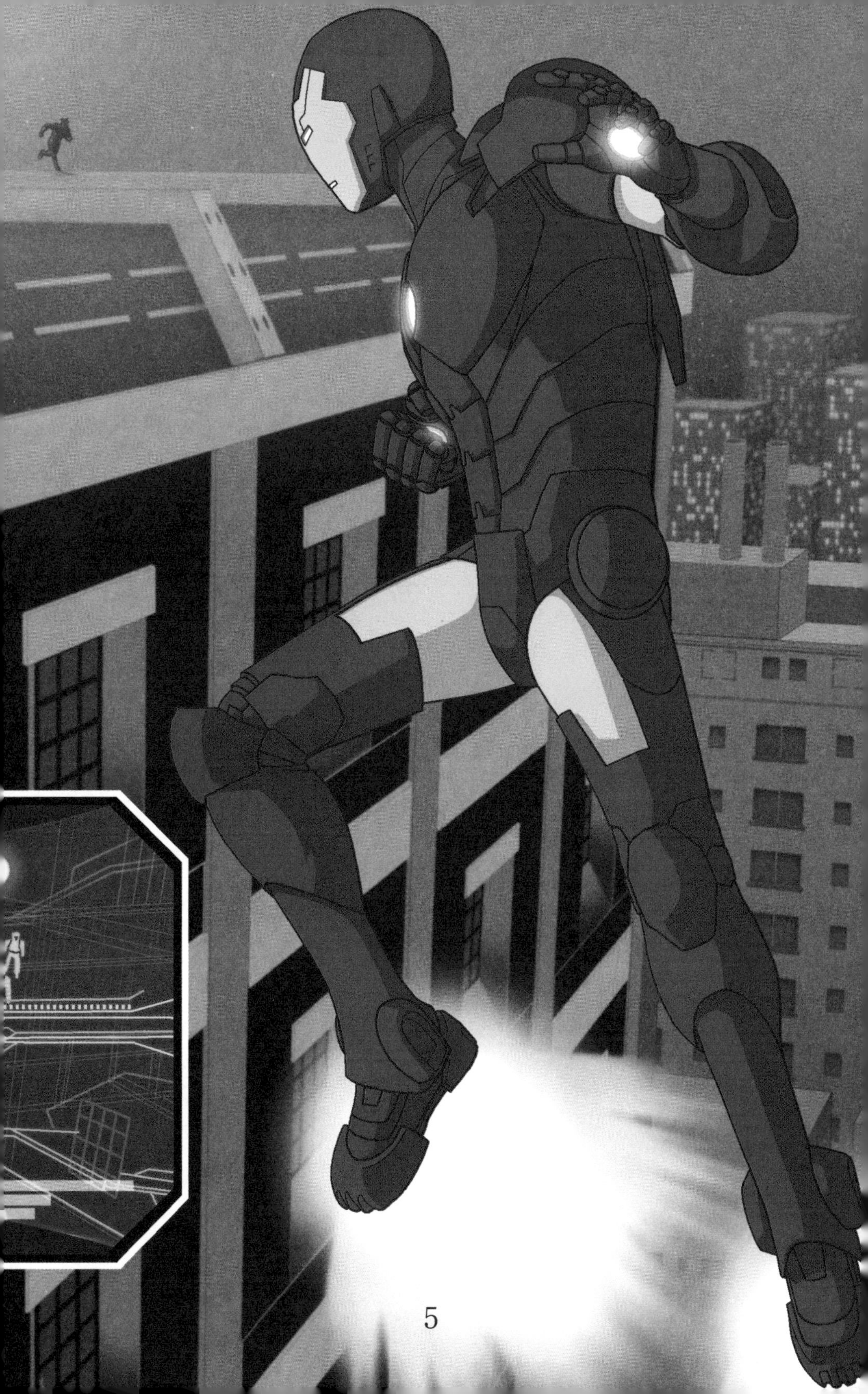

Suddenly, something
slammed into Iron Man!
It moved fast.
He only saw a blur.

It was a man dressed
as a big black cat!
"Bad kitty,"
Iron Man said.

The man lashed out
at Iron Man with sharp claws.
He cut Iron Man's armor!

"What are those claws
made of?"
said Iron Man.

An A.I.M. airship appeared.
The soldiers fired
at the man.

He jumped and dodged.
Then one shot destroyed
the roof of the building!

Iron Man raced at full speed
and saved the man from falling
to the ground.

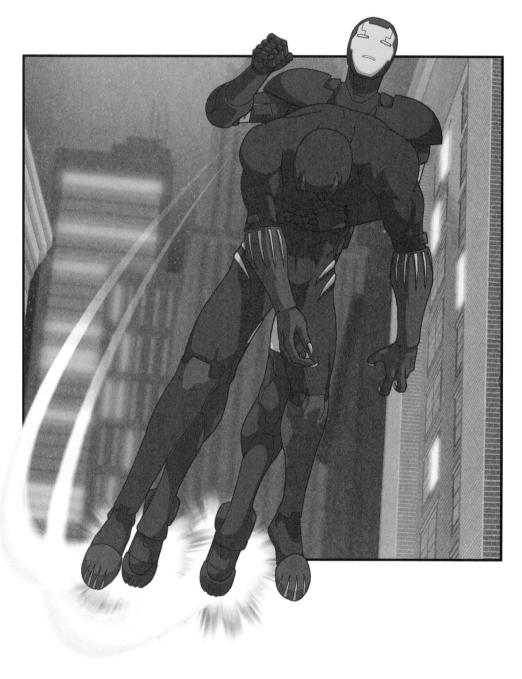

Iron Man took the stranger
back to his secret lab.
It was called the Armory.

Iron Man's friends
Rhodey and Pepper
helped the man.
"Why is he dressed like a black cat?"
Pepper asked.

"Not a cat,"

Rhodey answered.

"A *panther*. The king of Wakanda

is called the Black Panther!"

"The African nation
of Wakanda
was invaded last week,"
Rhodey said.
"The king was killed."

"Then who is this guy?"

Pepper asked.

"He's not much older than us."

Suddenly,
the Black Panther
stood up. He said,
"I am the *new*
king of Wakanda.

A man named Magnum
stole something from my country.
And I want it back."

"Magnum is dealing
with a group called A.I.M.,"
Rhodey said.
"We could work together
to stop both of them,"
Tony added.

The Black Panther
did not like that idea.
He warned Iron Man and his friends
to leave him alone.

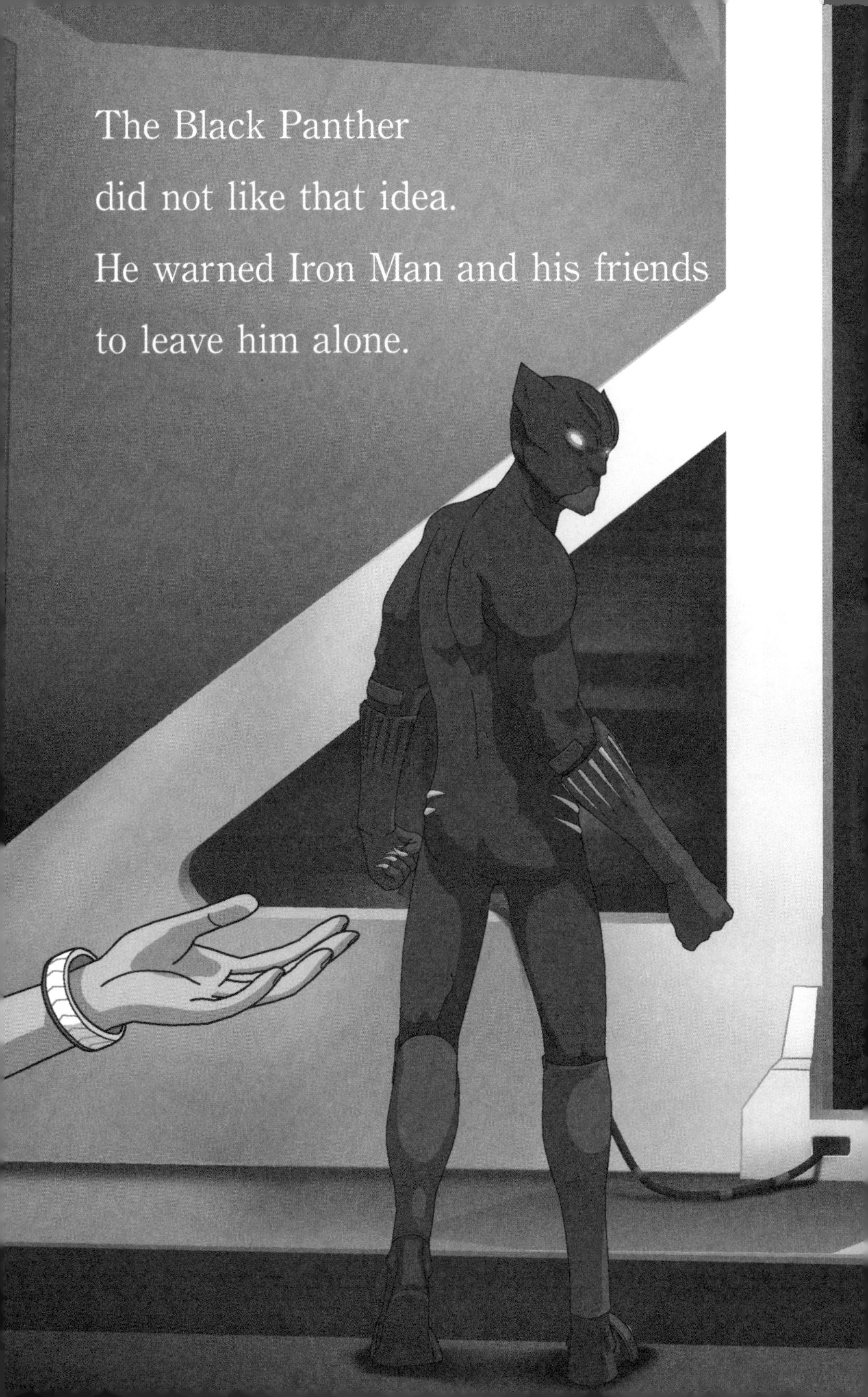

Just then,

the computer alarm rang.

A.I.M.—and Magnum—were on the move!

Iron Man and his friends learned
that Magnum was selling vibranium
to A.I.M.

"What's vibranium?"
Pepper asked.

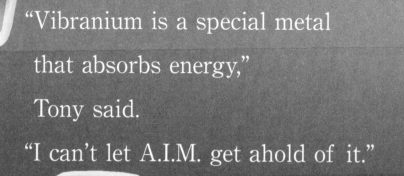

"Vibranium is a special metal that absorbs energy," Tony said.

"I can't let A.I.M. get ahold of it."

Pepper told Tony
to be careful.

Iron Man took off into the sky.

He was determined to stop A.I.M.

Iron Man found A.I.M.
on a bridge,
already fighting
the Black Panther!

The A.I.M. soldiers surrounded the Black Panther. But he was too fast and too strong for them!

He easily defeated the soldiers
with some kicks and a few
other quick moves.

Just then, Magnum arrived.

"Face me, Magnum!"

shouted the Black Panther.

The Black Panther lunged at

the evil man.

The stolen vibranium

was in Magnum's briefcase.

But the Black Panther
was struck by energy blasts
from more A.I.M. soldiers!

The vibranium

in the Black Panther's costume

began to absorb the energy!

Iron Man knew the vibranium
in Black Panther's suit
was about to explode.
He had to help him!

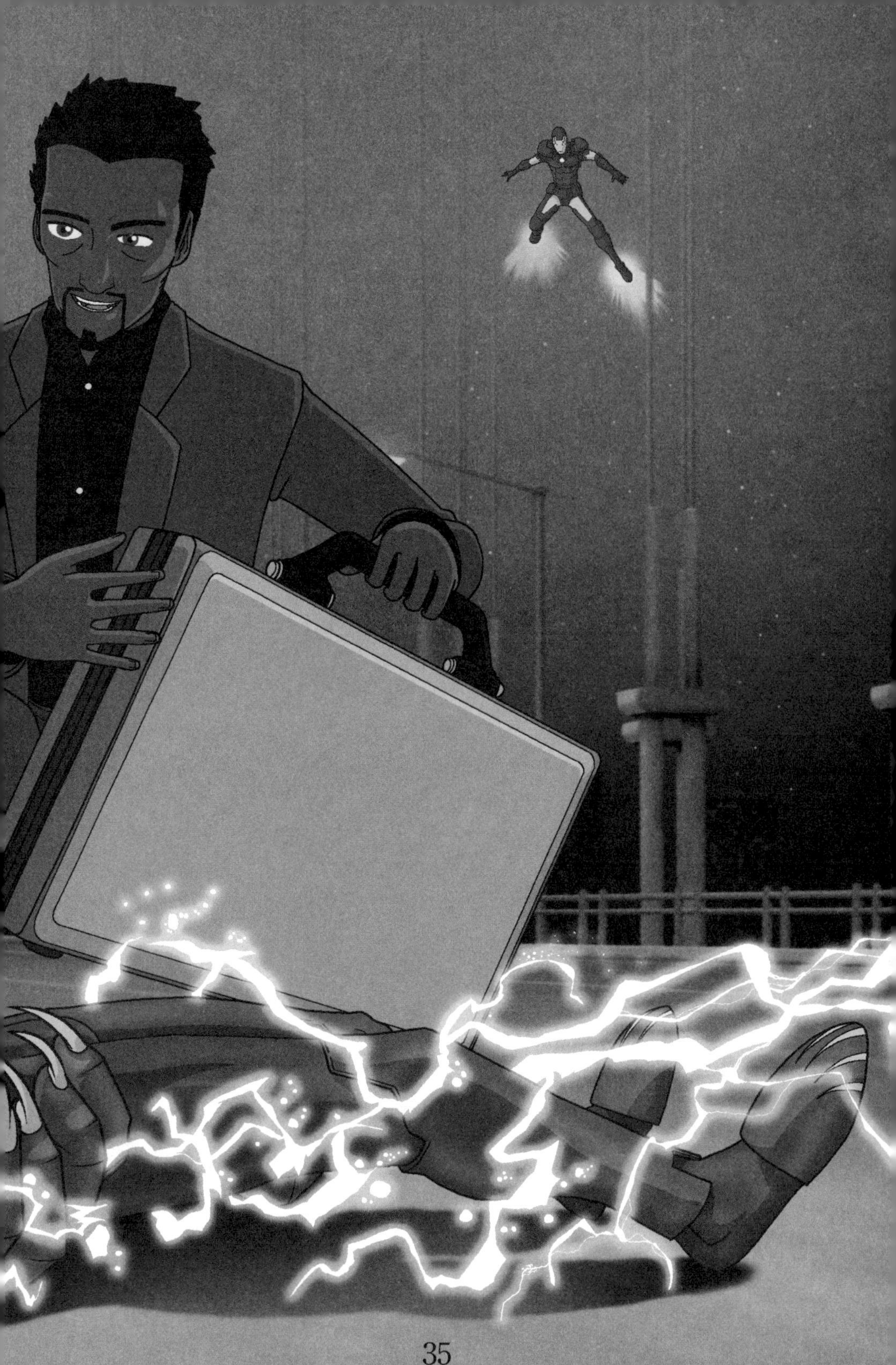

Iron Man rocketed
to the rescue.
He easily knocked over
the A.I.M. soldiers.

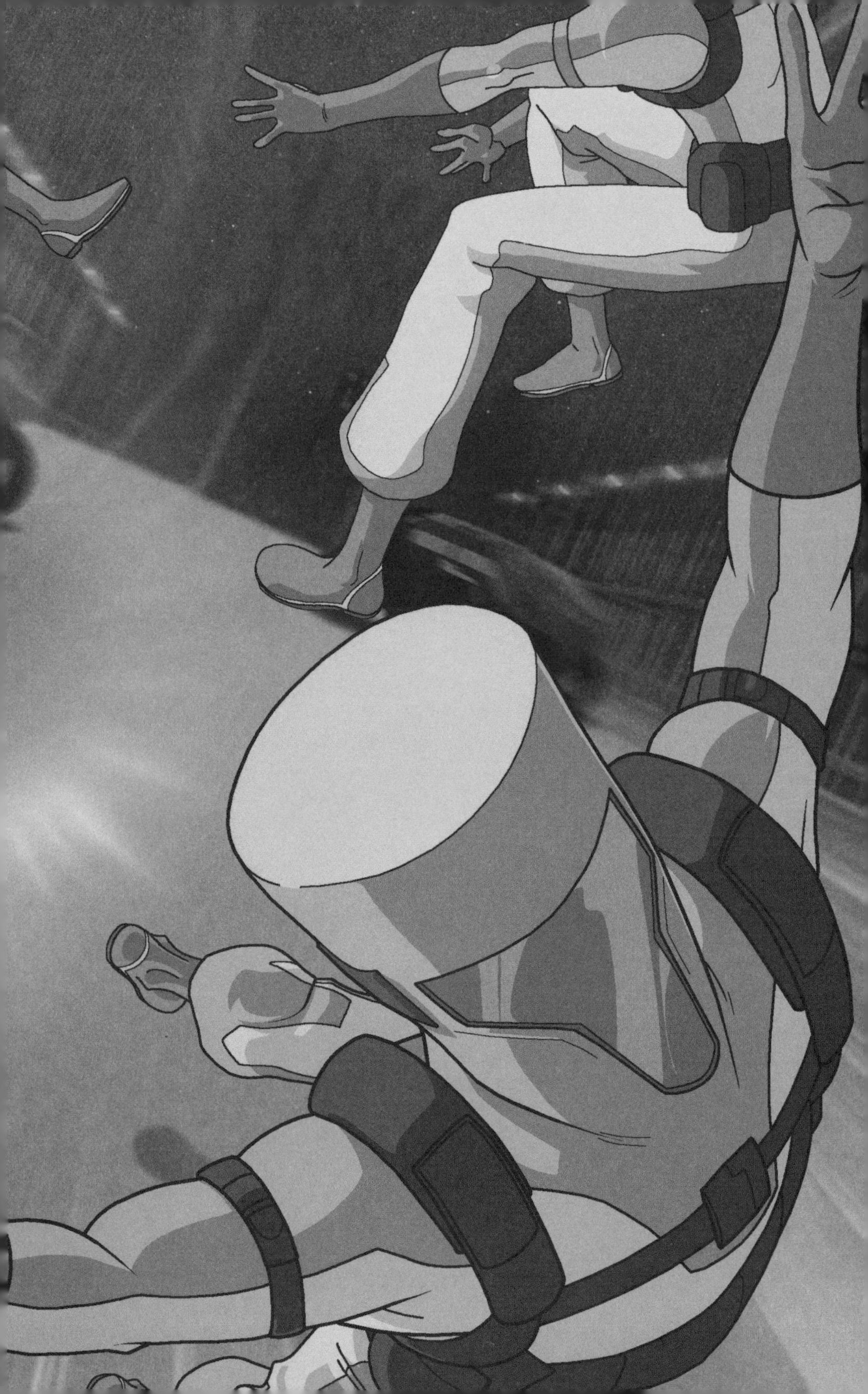

Iron Man helped
the Black Panther to his feet.
The Black Panther's suit
crackled with energy.

"You must go!"

the Black Panther warned.

"I'm going to explode!"

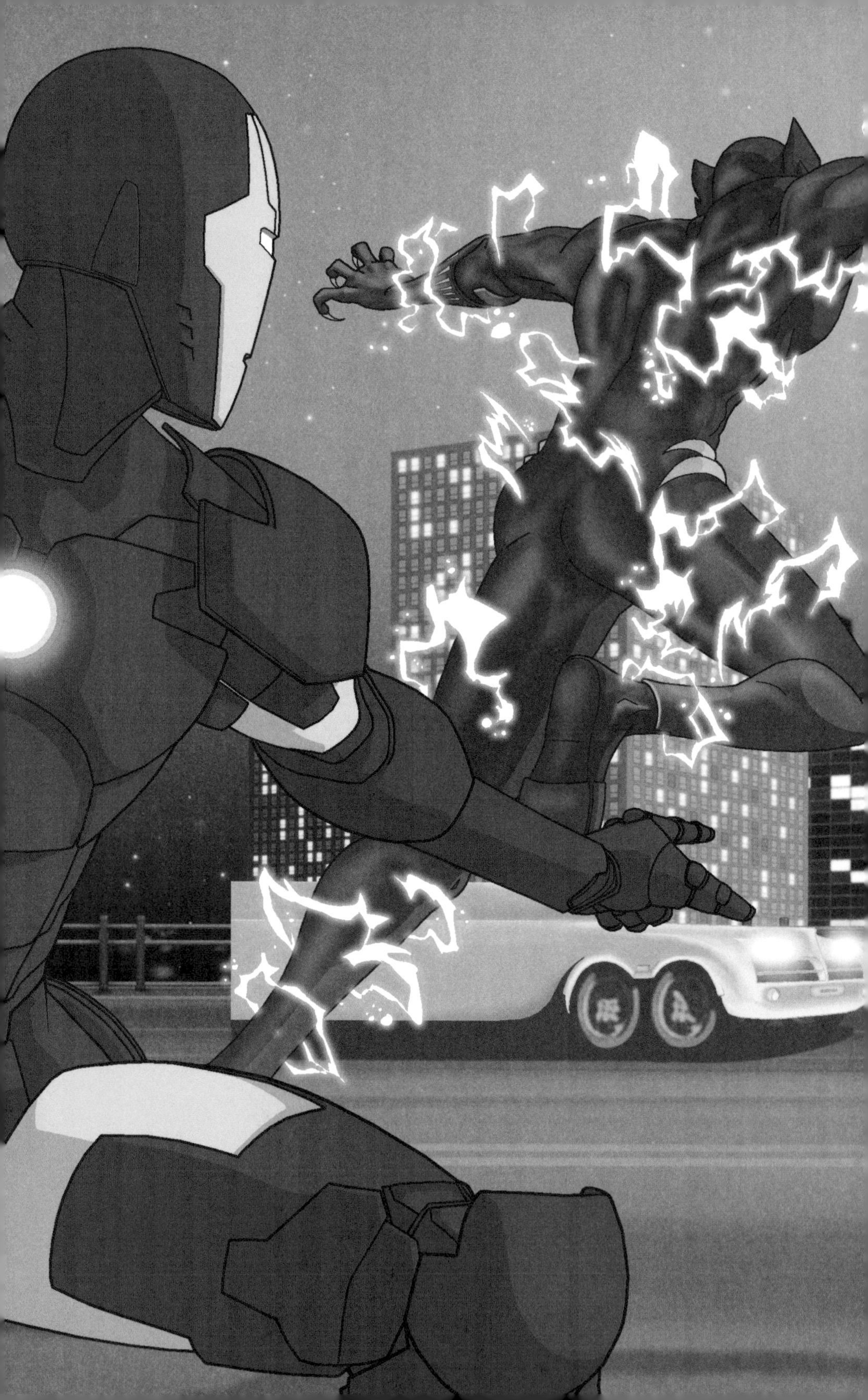

"You need to release the energy," Iron Man said.

The Black Panther nodded.

He pounced on the A.I.M. soldiers.

The Black Panther jumped
from soldier to soldier.
Each time he knocked one man down,
he released more energy from his suit!

The energy was quickly

used up.

The Black Panther was safe.

Next, the Black Panther
grabbed Magnum.
"I am taking you to face
Wakandan justice,"
he said.

Iron Man returned

the stolen vibranium

to the Black Panther.

"It helps to have friends,"
said Iron Man.
"You don't have
to do this alone."

"My father would still be alive
if he had asked for help,"
said the Black Panther.
"Perhaps *this* king
can change his ways."

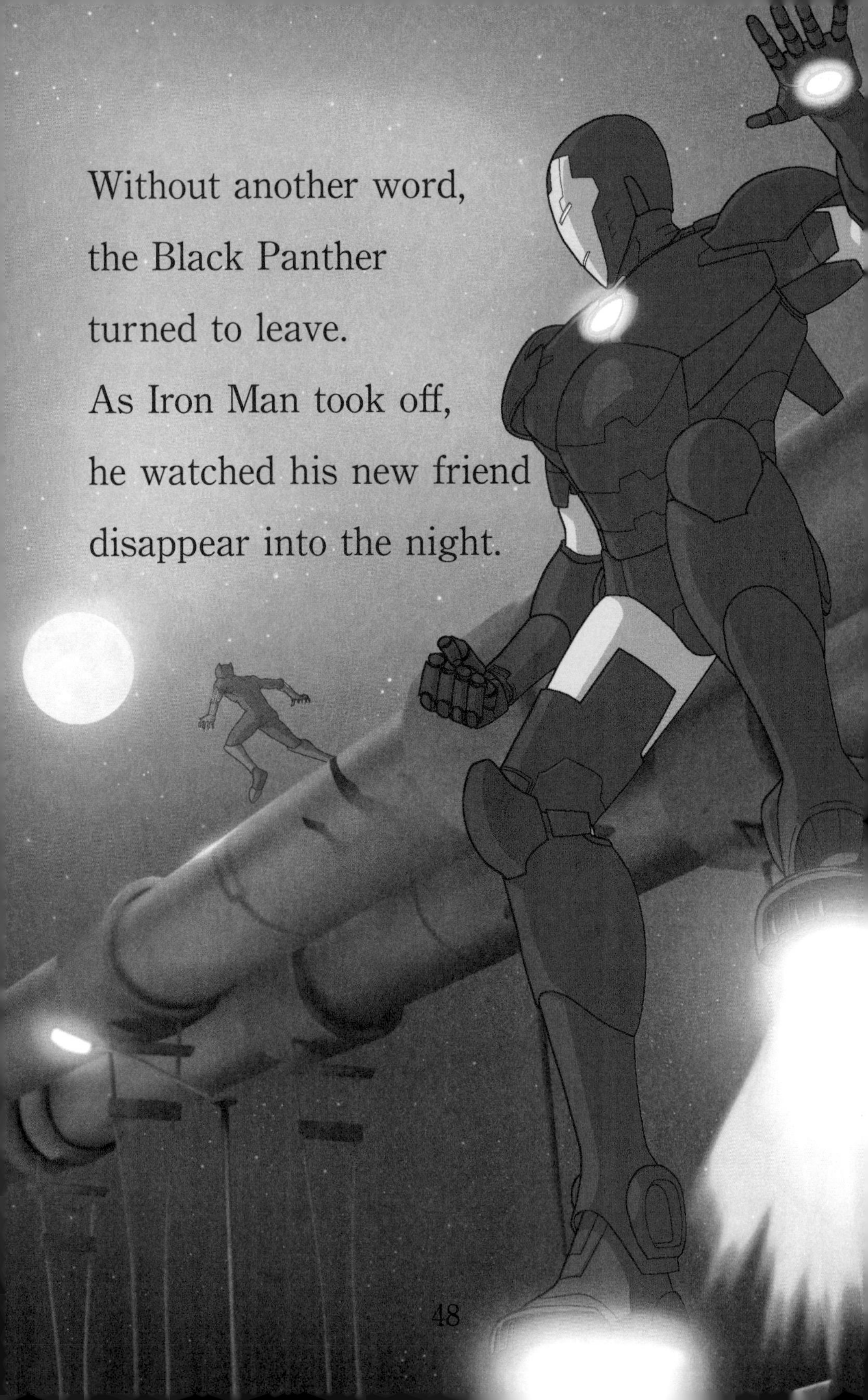

Without another word,
the Black Panther
turned to leave.
As Iron Man took off,
he watched his new friend
disappear into the night.